PANCHATANTRA MORAL STORIES

VISHNU SHARMA

Stories from Mitralabha (Gaining Of Friends)

1. The Hermit and the Mouse

A hermit took care of a temple in a small village. He took alms and shared it with a few people who helped him clean the temple. There was a mouse in the temple that kept stealing the hermit's food and causing trouble for him. The hermit could not get rid of the mouse no matter what he did. The mouse continued to steal food, even when it was kept in an earthen pot hung from the roof.

Distraught, the sage sought advice from a friend, who told him to find the mouse's food reserves and destroy them. After a thorough search of the premises, the sage found the stockpile of the mouse and destroyed it. With its food gone, the mouse was unable to jump high up to the roof for food. It became weak and got caught by the hermit, who threw it far away from the temple. The mouse was hurt and never returned to the temple.

Moral: *Strike at the enemy's source of strength to defeat him.*

2. The Foolish Weaver

A weaver and his wife lived in a village. He went to the forest to get wood that he needed to repair his loom. As he began to chop the tree, a jinni appeared and asked him not to cut his abode. In return, the genie offered to give anything that the weaver wanted. The weaver left the forest to discuss this with his wife. The greedy and dimwitted wife told the weaver to ask the genie for an extra head and two extra hands so he can think more and work more.

The stupid weaver agreed and went back to the jinn, which immediately granted the wish. The weaver happily walked back to the village, where people thought him to be a monster and beat him to death.

Moral: *Lack of proper judgment can lead to several missed opportunities.*

3. Four Friends and a Hunter

A deer, a turtle, a crow and a rat were friends. They lived happily in a jungle. One day, the deer was caught in a hunter's trap and the friends made a plan to save him. The deer struggled as if it was in pain and then it lie motionless, with eyes wide open, as if it were dead. The crow and the other birds then sat on the deer and started poking it as they do to a dead animal.

Right then, the turtle crossed the hunter's path to distract him. The hunter left the deer, assuming it dead, and went after the turtle. Meanwhile, the rat chews open the net to free the deer while the crow picked up the turtle and quickly took it away from the hunter.

Moral: *Teamwork can achieve great results.*

Stories from Mitrabedha (Losing Of Friends)

4. The Jackal and the Drum

One day, a hungry jackal wandered into a deserted battlefield in search of food. The place had nothing but a drum that the army left behind. When the wind blew, the branches of a tree moved and hit the drum, making a loud noise. The jackal was scared and decided to run from there. On second thoughts, he decided to explore the noise. As he drew closer to the sound, he found the drum and realized that it was harmless. When he approached the drum, he found food nearby.

Moral: *Do not react blindly with fear.*

5. The Crows and the Cobra

Two crows, husband and wife, and a cobra lived on a banyan tree in a forest near a small kingdom. The cobra was wicked and ate the crows' eggs when the crows left the nest in search of food. The crows went to a wise jackal and ask for advice. As per the advice of the jackal, one of the crows went to the royal palace and stole a very precious necklace belonging to the queen as the guards watched. The crow flew slowly to its nest, so that the guards can follow it.

On reaching the banyan tree, the crow dropped the necklace in the tree's hollow cove, where the snake lived. On finding a cobra in the hollow, the guards killed it and retrieved the necklace. The crows thanked the jackal and lived happily.

Moral: *Even the most powerful enemies can be defeated with intelligence.*

6. The Lion and the Camel

In a dense jungle, a lion lived with its three assistants – a jackal, a crow and a leopard. Due to their proximity to the king of the jungle, the assistants never had to look for food. One day, they were surprised to see a camel, which usually lived in the desert, wandering in the forest. On inquiry, they learnt that the camel lost its way. The lion gave it shelter and protected it.

One day, the mighty lion was injured in a battle with the elephants. Unable to hunt, the lion and the assistants were left hungry. The three assistants suggested that they should eat the camel, but the lion refused to kill it. The assistants hatched a plan to make the camel offer itself as food to its protector. The crow, the leopard and the jackal each offered itself as food to the lion, which it refused. Seeing this, the camel also did the same and was instantly killed by the lion.

Moral: *It is unwise to trust cunning people who surround powerful or wealthy ones for their own benefit.*

7. Right-Mind and Wrong-Mind

Two friends, Dharmabuddhi (right, virtuous mind) and Papabuddhi (wrong, wicked mind) lived in a village. Papabuddhi, who was wicked, decided to use the skills of the virtuous Dharmabuddhi to make money. He convinced his friend to together travel the world and earn a lot of money. Once they earned enough money, Papabuddhi convinced his friend that they should bury the money in a forest for safety. He then stole all the money one night and went back to the village.

When the friends went back to the forest to get the money, Papabuddhi feigned ignorance, accused Dharmabuddhi of stealing the money and took the matter to the village elders, who agreed that they should ask the tree spirit in the forest about Dharmabuddhi's guilt.

Papabuddhi asked his father to hide in the tree bark and speak like the tree spirit to confirm the innocent man's guilt. Sensing something wrong, Dharmabuddhi set dry leaves and twigs on fire inside the hollow cove of the tree, forcing his friend's father out.

Papabuddhi's father confessed to his son's misdeed and the village elders punished him for it.

Moral: *Avoid association of the wicked or you may end up paying for their misdeeds.*

8. The Talkative Tortoise

Once upon a time, a tortoise named Kambugriva lived near a lake. It was friends with two swans that also lived in the lake. One summer, the lake began to dry up, and there was little water for the animals. The swans told the tortoise that there was another lake in another forest, where they should go to survive. They came up with a plan to take the tortoise along. They made the tortoise bite the center of a stick and told it not to open its mouth, no matter what.

The swans then held each end of the stick and flew, with the tortoise in between. People in the villages along the way saw a tortoise flying and were awestruck. There was a commotion on the ground about two birds taking a tortoise with the help of a stick. In spite of warnings from the swans, the tortoise opened its mouth and said: "what's that commotion all about?" And then, it fell to its death.

Moral: *One should speak only at the right moment.*

9. Goats and Jackal

A jackal was once passing by a village, when it saw two strong goats fighting with each other. The goats were surrounded by people who were cheering for them. A few minutes into the fight, the goats had bruises on the body and were bleeding a little. This jackal was drawn to the smell of blood and wanted to get a bite of the goats' flesh. It jumped at the goats at once, without thinking.

The two goats were stronger than the jackal and mercilessly trampled on the animal and killed it.

Moral: *Think before you jump.*

10. The Monkey and the Wedge

A team of carpenters was working on building a temple near a banyan tree. The carpenters went on a lunch break, leaving their tools and materials at the site. At this time, a group of monkeys came to the site and started playing with the tools and the material. One monkey found a huge log of wood with a wedge in it. A carpenter half-sawed a log and put a wedge to prevent the slit from closing.

The curious monkey settled inside the slit and tried to remove the wedge. After a lot of effort, it succeeded in removing the wedge. The slit closed instantly, injuring the monkey gravely and preventing it from moving from there.

Moral: *Interfering in other people's business results in more harm than good.*

11. The King and the Foolish Monkey

There was once a king who had a pet monkey. The monkey always accompanied the king and even did little chores for him. One afternoon, as the king took a nap, the monkey sat next to the king and fanned him. Meanwhile, a fly came and sat on the king's nose. The monkey tried to shoo it away, buy it kept coming back.

Frustrated with the fly, the monkey took the king's dagger to kill it. He attacked the fly as it sat on the king's neck, killing the king instantly.

Moral: *A fool can never assist you to glory.*

12. The Bug and the Poor Flea

A white flea lived between the silky sheets of a king. It fed on the king's blood without anyone noticing and was very happy. One day, a bug came by and expressed its desired to taste the king's blood. The flea was uncomfortable with the idea as the bug's sting can be painful and that could expose its presence to the king.

On the bug's insistence, the flea agreed that it can taste the king's blood but had to wait until after he went to sleep. The bug agreed but couldn't control itself. It bit the king as soon as he sat on the bed. The king was furious and asked the guards to check his bed for bugs. The bug quickly hid while the white flea got caught and killed.

Moral: *Do not trust the words of strangers, for they could just be false promises.*

13. The Crane and the Crab

An old and cunning crab had difficulty in catching fish. To avoid starvation, it came up with a plan to get food easily. It sat on the banks of the river with a sad face one day. On being asked, the crane said that he foresaw that there would be a famine, and all the animals in the pond would die soon. The naive fish believed the crane and sought its help. The crane happily agreed to carry the fish in its mouth and leave them in another lake near the mountains,

That way, the crane filled its stomach. One day it decided to eat a crab and carried it on its back. The crab saw a lot of fish skeletons on a barren land nearby and asked the crane about it. The crane confessed proudly that it ate all the fish and now it would eat the crab. The crab acted quickly on hearing this and used its claws to kill the crane and save its life.

Moral: *Do not believe hearsay; check the authenticity of the information before acting.*

Stories from Aparïksitakárakam (Imprudence)

14. The Musical Donkey

A washer man had a donkey named Udhata. The donkey carried loads during the day and was set free to graze in the nearby fields at night. He met a jackal one night and together, they would get food from nearby farms while the farmers slept. While Udhata enjoyed vegetables, the jackal attacked the farmer's poultry.

One night, Udhata was in a gay mood and told the jackal that he wanted to sing. The jackal warned him that singing while stealing vegetables from a farm is not a good idea. The donkey ignored the warning and sang to its heart's content, even as the jackal ran to save its life. Soon, farmers woke up hearing the donkey braying and beat it with sticks for eating the vegetables from their farms.

Moral: *There is a right time and place to do anything.*

15. The Bird with Two Heads

There was once a strange bird with two heads. Each head had a mind of its own. The bird had a very normal life, with the heads cooperating with each other for the bird's survival. One day, the heads started fighting for a fruit they saw on a tree. There was only one fruit, and each head wanted the fruit for itself. The second head suggested that they stop fighting and give the fruit to the wife instead.

Although the first head agreed, he was not happy and vowed to teach the first head a lesson. On finding a poisonous fruit, the first head offered it to the second head, which consumed it happily. Within minutes, the bird died leaving both the minds useless.

Moral: *This story has two morals: Having a conflicting state of mind is dangerous. And, every part of the body is important – loss of even one could be fatal.*

16. The Mongoose and the Brahmin's Wife

A brahmin, his wife, and his baby boy lived in a small village. They had a pet mongoose which lived with them. One day, when the brahmin was out on chores, his wife left the baby in the cradle and went to fetch a pot of water. She asked the mongoose to take care of the baby while she is away. As the mongoose guarded the baby, it saw a snake crawling into the house. It soon attacked the snake and killed it.

As soon as the brahmin's wife entered with the pot of water, the mongoose happily welcomed her with blood all over her mouth. The lady was terrified at the sight and assumed that the mongoose had killed the baby. Furious, the lady dropped the pot of water on the mongoose and beat it to death with a stick. Then she went inside and found the baby happily playing in the cradle.

The lady realized what she had done and repented for acting without thought.

Moral: *Do not act in haste without understanding the situation.*

17. The Tale of Two Fishes and a Frog

In a lake, there lived many fishes and frogs. Two fishes, Sahasrabuddhi and Satabuddhi, were friends with a frog called Ekabuddhi. They spent a lot of time together. One day, they overheard two fishermen talking about how the lake was a good spot for fishing. The fishermen decide to come back the next day for catching fish. Hearing this the frog decided to go away from the lake to save its life.

The fishes, however, were arrogant and refused to leave, saying that they can fool the fishermen with their swift movements and tricks. The frog left with its family and the next day, both Sahasrabuddhi and Satabuddhi were caught by the fishermen.

Moral: *Don't be overconfident in the face of danger, think of safety first.*

18. The Lion That Sprang To Life

In a village there lived four friends who were all brahmins. Of them, three were very gifted and had successfully learned the holy scriptures while the fourth one was not. One day, the friends decided to go to the king's court and show their skills and impress him. Although reluctant, the three brahmins agreed to take their dimwitted friend with them.

As they passed through a forest, they saw the carcass of a lion. Boastful of their skills, the three learned brahmins challenge one another and decided to bring the lion back to life with each of their skills. The fourth friend pointed out that it can be a dangerous idea. They brushed his opinion aside anyway. Scared of what was about to happen, the fourth friend quickly climbed a tree. As soon as the lion sprang back to life, it killed all the three brahmins and ate them.

Moral: *Common sense is always better than knowledge.*

19. The Brahmin's Dream

Once upon a time, there lived a poor brahmin without any friends or relatives. He was a miser and begged alms for a living. One day, he received a pot full of porridge by a generous person. He hanged the earthen pot from the wall and fell asleep staring at it. He drifted into deep sleep and dreamt that there was a famine, and that he exchanged his pot of porridge for a hundred gold coins.

He dreamt that he bought a pair of goats and cows with the money, and made more money by trading milk. He also dreamt that a rich merchant offered his daughter's hand in marriage and that he had a kid. He was relaxing at home when a group of kids would disturb him. Imagining that he was scaring them away with a stick, he picks up the nearby stick in his sleep and starts waving it around.

The brahmin wakes up suddenly, feeling the porridge on his hands and feet. He realizes that he had destroyed the only food he had for the day and repents his actions.

Moral: *Do not build castles in the air.*

Stories from Kákolùkïyam (Of Crows and Owls)

20. Elephants and Hares

A herd of mighty elephants lived in a dense forest. The elephant herd always occupied the little pond in the jungle, making it impossible for the other animals to drink water. The king of the hares approached the elephant king and presented the problem. The elephant dismissed him rudely.

To teach the elephant a lesson, the hare warns the elephant that the god of the lake, the moon, is unhappy with the elephant's behavior. The elephant did not believe the hare's words and asked to be taken to the moon god. The hare took the elephant to the lake on a full moon night and showed the reflection of the moon. Seeing that, the elephant believed that the moon god descended to the earth to punish them and agreed to change his herd's behavior.

Moral: *A little ingenuity can solve a seemingly big problem.*

21. The Foolish Brahmin and the Crooks

A Brahmin once performed sacred ceremonies for a rich merchant and got a goat in return. He was on his way back carrying the goat on his shoulders when three crooks saw him and decided to trick him into giving the goat to them. One after the other, the three crooks crossed the Brahmin's path and asked him the same question – "O Brahmin, why do you carry a dog on your back?"

The foolish Brahmin thought that he must indeed be carrying a dog if three people have told him so. Without even bothering to look at the animal, he let the goat go.

Moral: *If a lie is repeated several times, it becomes the truth for a fool.*

22. The Cave That Talked

A hungry lion wandered along the jungle it ruled in search of food. It was almost evening but the lion could not find a single animal to prey upon. Dejected, it decided to go back home, when it found a cave. The lion waited there for the resident animal to come back after sunset. He quickly went into the cave and hid.

The cave belonged to a jackal, which noticed the lion's paw prints as it entered.

He stepped back immediately and wanted to know if the lion was really inside its cave. The jackal made a plan to trick the lion. He started talking to the cave, asking if it was safe for it to enter. He kept asking the same thing again and again and refused to enter the cave until he got a reply.

The lion, fearing that his prey would walk away, replied like the cave. As soon the lion replied, the jackal ran away from the cave never to come back.

Moral: *Presence of mind can save you from being destroyed by foolish enemies.*

23. Crows and Owls

The birds of the jungle gathered for a meeting to discuss an important point. All birds, except the crows, showed up. The birds wanted to choose a new king as their present king, Garuda, was too busy and did nothing to protect them. After some thought, the birds agreed that the owl can see at night and should be made the king.

On the day of the coronation, a crow came and questioned the birds why they chose the owl as their king. On hearing the argument, the crow pointed out the flaws in the owl and suggested that Garuda should remain the king. The coronation was canceled and the owl, which was disappointed, declared that owls and crows shall never be friends. The crow repented giving unsolicited advice and flew away.

Moral: *Do not offer counsel unless asked for.*

24. The Thief, the Brahmin, and the Demon

A rich merchant was moved by the plight of a poor brahmin in his village and donated two calves to him. The brahmin was thankful and took good care of the calves, which soon became strong bullocks. The brahmin plowed his land with the help of these bullocks and earned a livelihood.

In the same village were a thief and a demon who wanted the bullocks for themselves. One night the thief and the demon came to the brahmin's house and got into an argument about who should have the animals. Their quarrel woke the brahmin, who started chanting sacred mantra on seeing the demons. The demon ran away, and the thief was chased away by the brahmin.

Moral: *When two people fight, it is always the third person who benefits.*

Stories from Labdhapranásam (Loss of Gains)

25. The Story of the Potter

A poor potter lived in a small village. One day, he fell into a ditch by accident and got hurt. The wound left a big scar on his forehead. The potter moved to another village when his village was affected by famine. Luckily, he got work in the king's court. The king saw the scar on the potter's face and assumed that he was a warrior. He treated the potter with respects and made him a prominent member of his court.

In the following months, the kingdom was attacked by the enemies and the king asked the potter to lead the army. Afraid to do so, the potter told the king the truth about himself and how he got the scar. The potter left the kingdom, leaving the king embarrassed.

Moral: *Appearances can be deceptive or never judge a person by his or her appearance.*

These stories will make your child ask for more and lure him into the habit of reading.

Made in the USA
Monee, IL
07 April 2022

94222835R00042